BOOK CLUB IN A BOX

Bookclub-in-a-Box presents the discussion companion for Khaled Hosseini's novel

THE KITE RUNNER

Published by Anchor Canada, a division of Random House of Canada Ltd., 2004. ISBN: 0-385-66007-3

Quotations used in this guide have been taken from the text of the hardcover edition of **The Kite Runner**. All information taken from other sources is acknowledged.

This discussion companion for **The Kite Runner** has been prepared and written by Marilyn Herbert, originator of Bookclub-in-a-Box. Marilyn Herbert. B.Ed., is a teacher, librarian, speaker and writer. Bookclub-in-a-Box is a unique guide to current fiction and classic literature intended for book club discussions, educational study seminars, and personal pleasure. For more information about the Bookclub-in-a-Box team, visit our website.

Bookclub-in-a-Box discussion companion for The Kite Runner

ISBN 10: 1-897082-28-2
ISBN 13: 9781897082287

This guide reflects the perspective of the Bookclub-in-a-Box team and is the sole property of Bookclub-in-a-Box.

©2005 BOOKCLUB-IN-A-BOX
©2008 2ND EDITION - JL

Unauthorized reproduction of this book or its contents for republication in whole or in part is strictly prohibited.

CONTACT INFORMATION: SEE BACK COVER.

BOOKCLUB-IN-A-BOX
Khaled Hosseini's The Kite Runner

READERS AND LEADERS GUIDE 2

INTRODUCTION

Suggested Beginnings 7

Novel Quickline 10

Keys to the Novel 11

Author Information 12

BACKGROUND INFORMATION

Afghanistan (A Portrait) ..17

Sunni, Shi'a Muslims 19

Taliban, Americans 20

CHARACTERIZATION

Amir and Hassan 23

Amir 24

Hassan 26

Baba 28

Rahim Khan, Ali 30

Assef 31

Gen. Taheri, Soraya 32

Sohrab 33

FOCUS POINTS AND THEMES

Faces of Afghanistan 38

Relationships 39

Friendship, Loyalty, etc 41

Guilt, Free Will, etc 43

Redemption 45

WRITING STYLE AND STRUCTURE

Filmic Quality 49

Exaggeration and Cliché ...50

Irony 51

Setting 52

SYMBOLS

Kite 57

Cleft 59

Dreams 59

Lamb, Sacrifice 61

Blood 62

LAST THOUGHTS 67

FROM THE NOVEL (QUOTES) ...71

ACKNOWLEDGEMENTS 81

BOOKCLUB-IN-A-BOX
Readers and Leaders Guide

Each Bookclub-in-a-Box guide is clearly and effectively organized to give you information and ideas for a lively discussion, as well as to present the major highlights of the novel. The format, with a Table of Contents, allows you to pick and choose the specific points you wish to talk about. It does not have to be used in any prescribed order. In fact, it is meant to support, not determine, your discussion.

You Choose What to Use.

You may find that some information is repeated in more than one section and may be cross-referenced so as to provide insight on the same idea from different angles.

The guide is formatted to give you extra space to make your own notes.

How to Begin

Relax and look forward to enjoying your bookclub.

With Bookclub-in-a-Box as your behind the scenes support, there is little for you to do in the way of preparation.

Some readers like to review the guide after reading the novel; some before. Either way, the guide is all you will need as a companion for your discussion. You may find that the guide's interpretation, information, and background have sparked other ideas not included.

Having read the novel and armed with Bookclub-in-a-Box, you will be well prepared to lead or guide or listen to the discussion at hand.

Lastly, if you need some more 'hands-on' support, feel free to contact us. (See Contact Information)

What to Look For

Each Bookclub-in-a-Box guide is divided into easy-to-use sections, which include points on characters, themes, writing style and structure, literary or historical background, author information, and other pertinent features unique to the novel being discussed. These may vary slightly from guide to guide.

INTERPRETATION OF EACH NOVEL REFLECTS THE PERSPECTIVE OF THE BOOKCLUB-IN-A-BOX TEAM.

Do We Need to Agree?
THE ANSWER TO THIS QUESTION IS NO.

If we have sparked a discussion or a debate on certain points, then we are happy. We invite you to share your group's alternative findings and experiences with us. You can respond on-line at our website or contact us through our Contact Information. We would love to hear from you.

Discussion Starters

There are as many ways to begin a bookclub discussion as there are members in your group. If you are an experienced group, you will already have your favorite ways to begin. If you are a newly formed group or a group looking for new ideas, here are some suggestions.

Ask for people's impressions of the novel. (This will give you some idea about which parts of the unit to focus on.)

- Identify a favorite or major character.
- Identify a favorite or major idea.
- Begin with a powerful or pertinent quote. (not necessarily from the novel)
- Discuss the historical information of the novel. (not applicable to all novels)
- If this author is familiar to the group, discuss the range of his/her work and where this novel stands in that range.
- Use the discussion topics and questions in the Bookclub-in-a-Box guide.

If you have further suggestions for discussion starters, be sure to share them with us and we will share them with others.

Above All, Enjoy Yourselves

INTRODUCTION

Suggested Beginnings

Novel Quickline

Keys to the Novel

Author Information

INTRODUCTION

Suggested Beginnings

1. The novel, **The Kite Runner,** is publicized as the first book written in English about Afghanistan. It tells a fascinating story about a culture and country which to date has been viewed through stereotype and misconceptions. The perspective has been political rather than personal. Yet Hosseini chooses deliberately to tell his story in cliché.
Discuss your thoughts about his choice of descriptive style. Has he succeeded in dispelling the stereotypes and misconceptions?

2. Baba's primary lesson to Amir is not to steal a man's right to the truth. Theft of the truth comes in many forms – Baba himself has stolen the truth from both his sons – Amir and Hassan.
Amir believes that Baba is angry with him because his mother died giving birth to him. Is Baba angry with Amir or with himself? How could he continue to rage on about "truth" when he himself did not practice it? Can this be justified?

3. Hosseini makes reference to the Kabul of the past as *"a strange world, one in which some things mattered more than the truth."* (p.315)

What matters more than truth? Are there reasons other than culture and the times that could account for Baba's lies? What would have changed had Baba told the boys the truth? Connect this discussion to the previous question.

4. By the time Baba and Amir leave Afghanistan, their whole life is reduced to two suitcases. This can be every immigrant's story, but the suitcases contain more than objects and clothes.

Discuss the tangible and intangible things that are contained within the suitcases.

5. In the Vietnamese grocery store, Baba becomes very angry when the owner, who has known him for two years, asks him for identification. Ironically, the owner is a Vietnamese immigrant demanding this of an Afghani immigrant.

Is this a typical experience for immigrants? Are there other "typical" immigrant stories to discover or share?

6. Among the strange events that occur when Amir returns to Kabul in search of Sohrab is the encounter with the beggar who knew his mother. Amir tells us that this improbable incident is believable because, in Kabul, *"absurdity was commonplace."* (p.263)

In the west, we speak of "six-degrees of separation," but is it possible to believe in such absurd improbabilities? Does this scene (or others in the story) contribute to or detract from your enjoyment of the novel?

7. Guilt is an emotion felt by both Amir and Baba, and perhaps by Rahim Khan as well. Rahim Khan tells Amir that redemption is always possible: *"there is a way to be good again."* He justifies Baba's actions by describing the good deeds Baba did, for example, building the orphanage.

Is Rahim Khan correct when he says that redemption is the result of guilt creating good deeds? (p.316) **Discuss Baba, Amir and Rahim Khan in this light.**

8. In Ontario, Canada, the provincial government has looked to, but rejected, shari'a law (the laws which instruct the Islamic way of life) as a way for the community to self-manage its affairs.

Given the novel's descriptions of how shari'a law is applied by the Taliban, is such proposed legislation reasonable? Desirable?

9. The feminine point of view is absent in this story about motherless families. The women are either missing or as powerless as Soraya's mother.

Is Soraya the exception? Does she add to or temper the novel's masculine perspective, or not? Is this something Hosseini overlooked or did intentionally?

10. Imagine if, as a child or adolescent, you suddenly had (or already have had) to leave the home of your birth, as did Amir and Hosseini.

What images and memories would stay with you into adulthood?

11. Baba's stated theory that the only sin of consequence is "theft" haunts Amir throughout his life and influences his behavior and self-image. (see Baba, p.28)

What is the truth of this theory? Can a parent's personal outlook have a devastatingly negative (or positive) effect on a child?

12. *"One thousand times over"* is Hassan's expression of loyalty and friendship.

What are some other common expressions used to convey loyalty and friendship in different cultures?

There are many wonderful scenes in this novel. Which is your favorite? Is it possible to pick only one?

Novel Quickline

- The story of **The Kite Runner** is set in the extremely turbulent country of Afghanistan, spanning more or less three unsettling decades in its history – from the early 1970s, when the monarchy is ousted in a bloodless coup (1979), to the period of Taliban rule in the 1990s. The primary character is a boy, Amir, who has to deal with the tragic consequences of both his father's emotional rejection of him and of living in a society that is rife with conflict and prejudice. However, he finds that coming to terms with his own conscience is the greater challenge. He must accept his own actions, inactions and reactions to the vicious attack on his friend and servant, Hassan, that occurred on the day of Amir's greatest triumph – the day he won the kite fight.

- This is the first novel written in English about Afghanistan and its author's goal is to: *"... humanize the Afghan people and put a personal face to what has happened there."* (Sadat) At the same time, the story has a universal appeal. It deals with difficult choices of conscience that people may face at some time in their lives and that are often heightened when those times are difficult and/or violent; it deals with issues of the father/son relationship, with issues of friendship, loyalty, courage and cowardice – in all forms; and finally, it speaks of the universal immigrant experience of attempting to create and build life anew within a foreign land and culture.

- The story begins when the boys are young and we witness the imbalance of their personal relationship juxtaposed with the unequal social status between Pashtuns and Hazaras. We witness the arrogance and disdain that Amir shows to Hassan, and the never-changing dignity with which Hassan receives this behavior. However, Amir is not all bad; he does suffer from a guilty conscience, and so the book deals with redemption as the way *"to be good again."*

- We follow the small motherless family through the "good times" in Kabul, then through a more difficult period in Pakistan while they make their way to a better life in America. Then, suddenly, we are once more thrown back into a very changed Afghanistan where Amir returns to make amends to Hassan, whom he has wronged.

- In the last section of the novel, many questions are answered, but new ones are also posed. Once Amir saves Sohrab, Hassan's son, he has much difficulty getting him into the United States. There is a great deal of political posturing and red tape. With this epigraph, Hosseini is addressing every immigrant with similar stories of struggle. In effect, Hosseini has gone beyond his goal of humanizing Afghanistan and creating a new understanding of her people. He is reaching out to the international community on behalf of those very people and is asking for a different level of action. There is a way for the world to *"be good again"* in its dealings with all individuals in need.

Keys to the Novel

Identity

- A key to reading this novel more effectively is to juxtapose the individual story of Amir and Hassan with the story of Afghanistan, the country. In both cases, there is a struggle for identity and the survival of that identity. The question becomes what do we destroy in the struggle to define the indefinable, in the struggle to change, adapt, and become something new.

Redemption

- Both individuals and countries seek the peace of redemption. It is possible in both cases, but only through the tremendous courage of self-examination. The key is to do this independently and alone. For Amir, it means having to wait until Baba dies and is no longer present for Amir to depend on.

- For Afghanistan, Hosseini implies that change and redemption too must come from within. Outside interference and dependency has led the country to the brink of destruction. In the fall of 2004, Afghanistan held its first democratic elections. The results brought together the many faces of Afghanistan – the former military, the Taliban, women activists, and ex-communists – to serve in the new parliament.

- Just as **The Kite Runner** is left open-ended in terms of Amir's relationship with Sohrab, the state of Afghanistan's political future remains to be seen.

Author Information

- Khaled Hosseini was born the oldest of five children in Kabul, Afghanistan, in 1965. His mother was a teacher at a girls' high school and taught Farsi and History; his father was a diplomat in the Afghan Foreign Ministry, which necessitated living in three different countries in a time-span of ten years.

- In 1976, during a period of relative calm in Afghanistan, the family moved to Paris, France, where Hosseini's father was assigned a post in the Afghani embassy. They were due to return to Afghanistan in 1980, but by then the Soviets had invaded the country. The family was granted political asylum in the United States. Khaled was 11 years old when he moved to San Jose, California.

- As for many immigrants, life for the Hosseinis was predictably difficult economically, linguistically, socially, and culturally, but they were delighted with their new country and persevered. Khaled earned an undergraduate degree in biology from Santa Clara University and then graduated from the University of California School of Medicine at San Diego in 1993.

- He has been practicing internal medicine in the San Francisco Bay area since 1996 but finds time for his second love, a parallel career, as a writer. He rises each morning at 4 am to write and then goes off to the second part of his day to serve his medical patients. He is wonderful at multi-tasking and has a variety of eclectic interests.

- He has been noted or rewarded as a new writer by retail literary groups such as Barnes and Noble and Borders; he has been hailed by newspaper publishers such as Entertainment Weekly and the San Francisco Chronicle; he was given the Boeke Prize, a new award given by a South African bookstore chain for a novel's readability and entertainment factors; and the Alex Award, which highlights adult books suitable for and of interest to young readers. **The Kite Runner**, his first novel, remains high on all best-seller lists.

- Hosseini is married with two young children, a boy (Haris) and a girl (Farah).

- Hosseini's vision for **The Kite Runner** is mostly fictional but is tinged with autobiographical elements – for example, he describes the first years spent on welfare and working at the flea market along with other Afghani immigrants before assimilating and succeeding in becoming an integrated member of the new American culture. Partly because of these struggles and partly because Afghanistan has been seen in the past in terms of its wars with the Soviet Union and the Taliban, Hosseini wanted to put together a more complete picture of life before these specific threatening events. And so, he introduces to Western culture a portrait of a cosmopolitan, artistic, and intellectual environment that was once Kabul. However, in 2007, the trouble continues.

- For his novel, Hosseini was inspired by the positive memories of his life before the Soviet invasion and the special memory of a friendship he had with a Hazara boy who lived with his family in those early years. Hosseini's reflections led him back to Afghanistan in 2003, to see what had become of his former country. He tells of being astounded by how similar his own thoughts and observations were to Amir's when he returns to Kabul to seek out Sohrab. The novel had already been placed in production, so his personal experiences at that time were not incorporated into it.

- Hosseini has written a second novel called **A Thousand Splendid Suns**. Like his previous novel, it is set in Afghanistan, but this time he shows the troubled country through the lives of two women and their experiences in this male-dominated society over a period of thirty years.

- As for **The Kite Runner**, Stephen Spielberg's Dream Works is getting ready to film and release a movie based on the novel. It will be directed by Marc Forster, who previously directed *Finding Neverland* and *Monster's Ball*.

BACKGROUND INFORMATION

Afghanistan

Sunni and Shi'a Muslims

The Taliban

BACKGROUND INFORMATION

Afghanistan   *a portrait*

- Afghanistan has two economies – one legal (agriculture) and the other illegal (the growth and exportation of the opium poppy). Afghanistan provides 70 percent of the world's opium and 90 percent of Europe's heroin. Yet Afghanistan today is one of the world's poorest countries. The world's largest numbers of refugees are the Afghanis – almost 5 million are displaced either internally or in Pakistan and Iran.

- In a population of almost 29 million people, the illiteracy rate is 50 percent in men and 70 percent in women; the average life expectancy is 43 years; 15,000 women die in child-birth or because of pregnancy-related issues yearly, and communication in this mountainous country is tenuous at best. There are fewer than 30,000 telephones in the entire country. In the years between 1998 and 2002, Afghanistan, with only 12 percent arable land, suffered the further indignity of severe drought. This complication and the result of years of war devastated an already ravaged and wasted country.

- Afghanistan is a country fragmented by a long history of foreign occupation and interference by the Persians, Greeks, Turks, Indians, British, and Russians. When foreign invaders were not present, Afghanistan became embroiled in fighting among its various tribes. The Taliban, which began as a group of fundamentalist Islamic students, formed the last wave of aggressors against the population, that is until 2001 when the Americans invaded and began to banish the Taliban. The word "talib" means "scholar."

- As each invader came, many stayed and settled. This resulted in the great diversity of culture and ethnicity that makes up the country. For example, Afghanistan, with its population of more than 27 million people, is divided into approximately twenty different ethnic groups, which are further divided into individual tribes. Thrown into this mixture come more than fifty individual languages and dialects of each group and subgroup.

- The Pashtuns, mostly Sunni Muslims, consider themselves to be the "true Afghans," the original settlers of Afghanistan. They form approximately 40 percent of the current population. As the dominant group, they fill the positions of power in the society.

- Next in number (25%) are the Tajiks, who originally come from Tajikistan, the country to the north of Afghanistan. The Tajiks are also Sunni Muslims and are educated and prominent in all levels of Afghani life, from farming to the economy to government. They rival the Pashtuns for dominance in the country.

- The Hazaras, who descend from the Mongol invaders of the 13th century, are third in number at 19 percent of the population.

- Hosseini reflects some of this history throughout the novel but concentrates on the relationship between the Pashtuns and Hazaras. This conflict and the interference of other states has seriously weakened an already impoverished Afghanistan. Hosseini successfully portrays the despair that Amir feels when he wonders whether the Afghani people will ever rise above their troubled history to become one strong and secure nation.

Sunni and Shi'a Muslims

- Like all religions, there are levels of observance ranging from moderate to orthodox. For the purposes of this guide, the groups are mentioned according to general category only. The Sunnis form the overwhelming majority of all Muslims in Afghanistan, approximately 80 percent. The Shi'a population is about 20 percent. The Hazaras are predominantly Shi'a.

- The distinction between the Sunni and Shi'a Muslims arises from the struggle for leadership after Muhammad's sudden death (from illness) in AD 632. Thus the initial split was a political, rather than a doctrinal one. The Taliban are Sunni Muslims, but the fundamentalists who took over in Iran in 1979 are Shi'a. Both groups operate from a strong and strict perspective of adherence to Islam.

- Baba, however, has his own prophetic perspective on the fundamentalist movement. *"You'll never learn anything of value from those bearded idiots ... Piss on the beards of all those self-righteous monkeys ... God help us all if Afghanistan ever falls into their hands ..."* (p.18) But, of course, it does, with predictably destructive results.

The Taliban

- During the Russian occupation, there were Afghans who were determined to keep their country independent. However, this group, the Mujahedin, consisted of a number and variety of fundamentalist Islamic sects, who lived in the mountains and in Pakistan, where some of them formed alliances with other, more extreme leaders who called for jihad (holy war). The Americans supported many of these groups, as they began to fear the Soviet domination of the region. They covertly supplied arms to these groups. Following the expulsion of the Russians by the Mujahedin, and a period of increasing internal division, the Taliban eventually emerged as the government. As Rahim Khan tells Amir, it was a move welcomed by the country at that time.

CHARACTERIZATION

Amir and Hassan

Amir

Hassan

Baba

Rahim Khan, Ali

Assef

Gen Taheri

Soraya

Sohrab

CHARACTERIZATION

In this novel, Hosseini faces the challenge of portraying some, but not all, of the different faces of Afghanistan. There are a variety of vivid characters whose function is primarily to be the vehicle through which Hosseini discusses his themes of loyalty, friendship, and the brotherhood of Afghanistan.

Amir and Hassan

- Amir and Hassan must be considered first together and then separately because their relationship is an entity unto itself. They are the two faces of Afghanistan, different, but indivisible. They are portrayed as if they were fraternal twins, and in fact, they are born to the same father and nursed by the same unknown woman – Afghanistan herself. The two boys represent the *"brotherhood between people who had fed from the same breast, a kinship that not even time [can] break."* (p.11)

- For each boy, his first words refer to their respective heroes, again the multiple faces of Afghanistan. For Amir, his hero is Baba; for Hassan, it is Amir. Their love is unquestioned and pure, but their champions are human, and by definition, imperfect, like Afghanistan. By emphasizing the flaws, Hosseini brings to the reader a reaction to the emotional impact of culture and faith, and includes his personal message that if change were to come to each character, it could only come from within, as a result of introspection. (see Last Thoughts, p.67)

- Amir shows the flaws and weaknesses of the ruling Pashtuns in juxtaposition to Hosseini's presentation of the courage, heroism and kindness represented by Hassan's Hazaras. With the boys, Hosseini is able to point out that dignity should be recognized as a human characteristic not belonging to any one particular group.
  (see Relationships, p.39)

- Both boys are sons of the same father, so why are they different? The message contained in this metaphor is that all Afghanis are brothers, despite their disparity, so forget the fight.

Amir

- Amir is Baba's legitimate child, born to his legal wife who then tragically dies in childbirth. This loss shapes Amir in a negative way, primarily because his father is conflicted about his relationship with Amir. To Amir, it seems that Baba wants to be proud of him, but is continually disappointed in his character and behavior. Amir feels that Baba is angry at him and, perhaps, blames him for the death of his mother. *"Did he ache for her, the way I ached for the mother I had never met?"* (p.7) As a parallel, Amir aches for his father, too, who is emotionally and metaphorically absent. (see Relationships, p.39)

- Amir is conflicted about his identity – he seems to share the softer qualities (love of reading and writing) with his mother, but he wants to be the strong and courageous sports-minded "man" that he senses his father would admire. No matter what he does, he can't seem to gain his father's approval. *"If I hadn't seen the doctor pull him out of my wife with my own eyes, I'd never believe he's my son."* (p.25) The closest he comes is his triumph in the kite flying contest.

- Amir wants to be a good person and is constantly horrified at his own moral shortcomings, most of which are connected to his relationship with Hassan. From the beginning, Amir acknowledges himself as an unattractive character. *"I became what I am at the age of 12, on a frigid overcast day in the winter of 1975."* (p.1) He is a cold and emotionally frozen character whose personality is matched by the weather. (see Guilt, p.43)

- An example of Amir's damaged personality is the way he is fascinated by his behavior towards Hassan. In fact, much of his self-loathing comes from how he teases Hassan mercilessly, *"[kind] of like when we used to play insect torture. Except now, he was the ant and I was holding the magnifying glass."* (p.57) The more aggressive Amir becomes, the more passively Hassan accepts it. Amir's behavior is no less abusive to Hassan than Assef's assault and rape. The physical damage may lessen over time, but the emotional damage remains.

- Amir is dictatorial, demanding, and decidedly difficult towards Hassan. Just like every typical bully, Amir's behavior escalates with Hassan's increasing submissiveness. He lies constantly to Hassan, Ali, Baba and to himself. He is selfish and continually lives up to Baba's image of him as *"a boy who won't stand up for himself becomes a man who can't stand up to anything"* (p.232) This is the crux of Amir – until he can face himself and his challenges with honesty, he will remain the selfish self-absorbed adult he has become. He needs to find redemption. (see Redemption, p.45)

- Amir is the representative lens of the Afghan community through which Hosseini looks at his love for his homeland (from within and without), the continuation of culture (Amir marries Soraya, an Afghani), the hard-working nature of the immigrant (he watches as Baba works his fingers to the bone and ruins his health working for Amir's success), and guilt (for having left both Hassan and Afghanistan out of his life).

Hassan

- Late in the novel, we discover, as does Amir, the shocking information that Hassan is Baba's other, illegitimate and, therefore, unacknowledged son. Hassan was born a year after Amir. Both boys have lost their mothers. However, Hassan's loss is more shameful. In a culture where a good name is everything, Sanaubar, his mother, runs off with a troupe of entertainers. But the shame really belongs to Baba. The times, the culture, the people do not allow Baba to admit his fatherhood to Hassan. All Baba can do for Hassan is treat him as an honored and treasured employee. He tries to include Hassan in everything, but this only irritates Amir, which leads to his offensive behavior towards Hassan.

- Hassan is always ready to play with Amir and together they have many adventures. One time they get into trouble with Assef who threatens Amir. Hassan defends him with his slingshot and warns that if any harm is to come to Amir, Assef would hereafter be known as *"one-eyed Assef."* (p.45) This comes true later. Unfortunately, when it is Amir's turn to protect Hassan, he lacks the courage of character and runs away leaving Hassan to suffer Assef's vengeance. Amir's decision is made weighing Hassan's value against the triumph of winning the kite fight and Baba's favor.

Nothing was free in this world. Maybe Hassan was the price I had to pay, the lamb I had to slay to win Baba. Was it a fair price? The answer floated to my conscious mind before I could thwart it: He was just a Hazara, wasn't he? (p.82)

- While Hassan has no value to Amir, Hassan's true nature is such that he accepts everything with love, including his lot in life and his treatment at the hands of Amir. *"If I asked, really asked, [thinks Amir] he wouldn't deny me."* At every opportunity, Hassan protects and serves Amir. He is faithful and loyal without reservation; he is everything that Amir is not. Perhaps what Amir senses as Baba's disappointment in him, is simply that he has to share Baba's love with Hassan. Amir's misfortune is that he does not understand the inherent nature of their relationship until it is too late. (see Relationships, p.39)

- Hassan has no education and cannot read or write. He depends on Amir to teach him, but Amir constantly cheats him. Still, *"Hassan [is] drawn to the mystery of words, seduced by a secret world forbidden to him."* (p.30) His favorite story is the Persian epic of Shahnamah, the story of Rostam and Sohrab. Hassan later names his son, Sohrab, in honor of this story. Amir never teaches Hassan how to read, yet, ironically, Hassan is responsible for Amir's discovery that that he loves to create his own stories, which are the very ones Hassan likes best.

- Hosseini had originally planned to make Hassan the main character, but he realized that Amir is a more complex, conflicted and troubled character, and as such, has more room for character development. There is the occasional insightful moment when Amir actually does look at Hassan. He sees that Hassan's face has changed. *"Maybe not changed, not really, but suddenly I had the feeling I was looking at two faces, the one I knew, the one that was my first memory, and another, a second face, this one lurking just beneath the surface."* (p.58) This repeated image is again the two faces of Afghanistan. (see Faces, p.38)

Baba

- Baba, Amir's father, is described as *"a force of nature,"* or from Amir's perspective, as *"Mr. Hurricane,"* a bear of a man. And, in fact, according to local legend Baba had *"once wrestled a black bear in Baluchistan with his bare hands."* (p.13) He has the scars to prove it, but the story could also be "laaf," a characteristic which describes the Afghani inclination to exaggerate. Amir is faced with the issue of whether he, as the son of such a strong, dominant and powerful character, is predetermined to be weak. How, and in what way, can Amir crawl out from his father's overpowering shadow? These questions consume Amir throughout the novel as he searches for the way to be good.

- Baba was married to Sofia Akrami (Amir's mother): an educated, beautiful, respected, virtuous woman who taught classic Farsi literature at the university, and as her legend states, was a descendant of a royal family. Amir has inherited her gentle, poetic nature and her love of books and reading. It is Rahim Khan, and not Baba, who encourages and supports Amir as a writer when Amir brings his first written story.

    > *Seconds plodded by, each separated from the next by an eternity. Air grew heavy, damp, almost solid. I was breathing bricks. Baba went on staring me down, and didn't offer to read.* (p.34)

- The sadness of Baba is that as a proud member of the Pashtun ruling class he feels he can create the world in the image he imagines. The exception is Amir, a cowardly disappointment in his father's eyes. The irony, as we find out later, is that Baba too is cowardly – he never confesses to either boy that Hassan is also his son. (see Irony, p.51)

- Baba's lesson to Amir is that there is only one sin in life – theft.

    When you kill a man, you steal a life ... You steal his wife's right to a husband, rob his children of a father. When you tell a lie, you steal someone's right to the truth. When you cheat, you steal the right to fairness. (p.19)

- This black and white view of the world disturbs Amir greatly because *"after all, I had killed his beloved wife, his beautiful princess ... The least I could have done was to have had the decency to have turned out a little more like him. But I hadn't turned out like him. Not at all."* (p.20) The result for Amir is that he *"can't love a person who lives that way without fearing him too. Maybe even hating him a little."* (p.16)

- Hosseini has drawn a wonderful portrait of how emigration affects a person such as Baba. Despite Baba's love for America and all things American, he can't flourish there. He can't go back to Afghanistan and he can't prosper in America. He develops an ulcer, and later cancer.

- In the end, Baba shows Amir that he has had moments of pride in his son. He gives Soraya the book of Amir's writings that he has kept secretly for many years. (p.182) Amir realizes then that *"how much of who I was, what I was, had been defined by Baba and the marks he had left on people's lives ... Baba couldn't show me the way anymore; I'd have to find it on my own."* (p.184) This moment, before he becomes aware of Rahim Khan's final request, sets Amir on his road to redemption. He is beginning to understand that what he thought was Baba's perspective of Amir, was really Amir's own self-perception. Amir is his own black bear and he has the emotional scars to prove it.

Rahim Khan

- Rahim Khan, Baba's best friend and business associate, is the only person, other than Hassan, to see and accept Amir as a real person, flaws and all. He supports him in his writing and later pushes him to action to save Sohrab. *"As always, it was Rahim Khan who rescued me."* (p.34)

- It is Rahim Khan who tells Amir that his very best literary achievement is irony. But there is another fact of irony in Amir's life which Amir is slow to understand, even as Hassan knows it instinctively. Amir must learn that all relationships are sacred and must be protected at all costs with dignity and loyalty. *"There is a way to be good again."* (p.202) (see Irony, p.51)

- When he knows for sure he is dying, Rahim Khan summons Amir back to Kabul. He discloses the secrets of Amir's family and asks him to rescue Sohrab, Hassan's son. In a letter to Amir, he tells him what happened to Hassan all those years ago. He is instrumental in absolving Amir of his guilty conscience. He tells him that *"a man who has no conscience, no goodness, does not suffer,"* and it is clear throughout the novel that Amir has, indeed, suffered. (p.315) But this does not totally redeem Amir; he must follow through on this information. He may be absolved of his past behavior, but if he does not rescue Sohrab, he will not be redeemed from his future.

Ali

- Ali, Hassan's father, grew up with Baba in the same house, in much the same way as Hassan and Amir. Ali was Hazara; Baba was Pashtun. Ali's Hazara parents were randomly killed by Pashtuns. Ali was the survivor and at the age of five was adopted into Baba's house by Baba's father who had been the judge at the trial of the perpetrators. Sohrab must have been about the same age when he was taken to the orphanage.

- The parallels do not end there. Ali is described as having a *"congenital paralysis of his lower facial muscles, a condition that rendered him unable to smile and left him perpetually grim-faced."* (p.8) Hassan has a birth defect as well; he was born with a cleft lip. While Ali and Hassan both have facial scars, Baba and Amir have scars of the heart.

- Ali is constantly harassed by the neighborhood children in a situation paralleling Afghanistan's history of Hazara persecution by the Pashtuns. When Amir reads about how his own people, the Pashtuns, had suppressed the Hazara with *"unspeakable violence"* (p.9), he is appalled but perpetuates the same philosophy in his treatment of Hassan. Both sets of boys should have been soulmates, brothers. They are the two faces of Afghanistan. (See Faces, p.38)

Assef

- Assef is the neighborhood bully who seems to generate more favor in Baba's eyes than does Amir. He is particularly good at sports and is the *"embodiment of every parent's dream, a strong, tall, well-dressed and well-mannered boy with talent and striking looks ..."* (p.103) But his eyes, the windows of his soul, betray him. Amir always believed that he saw glimpses of madness in those eyes. Perhaps Assef knows this to be true, for when Amir meets him again in Taliban-controlled Kabul, Assef is wearing dark sunglasses. (see Irony, p.51)

- Even as a young boy, Assef admired Hitler and his Nazi vision of a pure Aryan world. Assef fits perfectly into the Taliban world because he, too, has a vision for Afghanistan: Afghanistan for the Pashtuns, the "pure" Afghans. For this reason, Assef continually harasses Ali and Hassan and includes Amir in that persecution because Amir is not a strong representative of the Pashtun race and therefore can be set aside.

General Taheri

- General Taheri was part of the Ministry of Defense in the now deposed Afghanistan government. He sits with sad dignity at the flea market, refusing to work because he is always waiting to be called back to Afghanistan. Unlike Baba, the general has empty dreams and so has kept his family on welfare. However, this situation weighs heavily on his mind and the general suffers from migraine headaches and takes anti-depressants. (p.185)

- General Taheri has a number of functions in the novel, not the least of which is to have a daughter, Soraya, with whom Amir falls in love. The general's main purpose is to represent the Afghani perspective and outlook on women and children. His opinions may be common among many cultural groups.

- First, he prevents Soraya's mother (a once famous singer) from pursuing her music. She agrees because in that culture, *"[every] woman needed a husband. Even if he did silence the song in her."* (p.187) Secondly, he kidnaps Soraya back to her home after she runs away with a non-Afghani. There is resulting shame and rumor that hangs over the family. Thirdly, it is the general's opinions on adoption that paralyze Amir and Soraya in their relationship. It makes their subsequent relationship with Sohrab both difficult and important.
(see Blood, p.62)

Soraya

- Amir sees Soraya at the flea market and falls in love. *"I blinked, my heart quickening. She had thick black eyebrows that touched in the middle like the arched wings of a flying bird, and the gracefully hooked nose of a princess from old Persia – maybe that of Tahmineh, Rostam's wife and Sohrab's mother from the*

Shahnamah." (p.148) Ironically, she is fated to become Sohrab's adoptive mother.

- After her illicit affair and ignominious return home, she is no longer considered marriageable. Therefore, she is the perfect match for Amir who considers himself to be soiled and spoiled.

Sohrab

- Sohrab is the young son of Hassan, the nephew of Amir. When Amir sees him for the first time,

    the resemblance was breathtaking. Disorienting.

    The boy had his father's round moon face, his pointy stub of a chin ... [it] was the Chinese doll face of my childhood. (p.292, 293)

- Sohrab, the child, represents the vulnerable Afghanistan, offspring of a violent history that needs to be understood and rescued from those who would destroy her. Hosseini is clearly saying that the destruction is coming from within. (see Keys to the Novel, p.11)

FOCUS POINTS AND THEMES

Faces of Afghanistan

Relationships

Friendship, Loyalty, Humanity

Guilt, Free Will, Determinism

Redemption

FOCUS POINTS AND THEMES

Myths and stereotypes appear in people's conversations and consciousness when there are no facts to accompany them, and as a result, the facts can be distorted. For instance, it is commonly believed that Afghanistan is simply a nation of terrorists and opium traders. The novel is a wonderful tool in order to dispel myths such as these. The imagination and descriptive characteristics of fiction enable the author to humanize and personalize the people behind the stereotypes.

The Kite Runner, is Hosseini's look at the nature of both humanity and Afghanistan from within and without. He introduces us to the individual, moves through the relationships connecting them, and then concludes with a look at Afghanistan as a whole. Nothing is isolated in Hosseini's investigation, but all is connected and interconnected through relationships and perspective. He is looking at the faces of Afghanistan, one face at a time. He opens the discussion for Afghanis and non-Afghanis alike.

Faces of Afghanistan *the nature of the country*

- Hosseini begins by describing Amir's sudden observation that Hassan's face has changed.

    > *Maybe not changed, not really, but suddenly I had the feeling I was looking at two faces, the one I knew, the one that was my first memory, and another, a second face, this one lurking just beneath the surface.* (p.58)

    This repeated image represents the two faces of Afghanistan. Throughout Afghanistan's long and complicated history, there has never been a single defining feature that could identify a particular group as being pure Afghani. The Pashtuns have tried to claim that distinction based on their numbers, their strength and the length of time they have been in Afghanistan. Hosseini disputes their position and claims that the true Afghanistan is made up of many different faces and many relationships.

- After September 11, the Americans invaded Afghanistan as a response to the destruction of the New York World Trade Center. Hosseini doesn't criticize this action, but laments the bombing of a country that has already been stripped and devastated by the Taliban. Hosseini believes that what Afghanistan needs is food and sympathy, not war. On some level, Hosseini is promoting understanding between America and Afghanistan, as well as between Afghanis themselves. As a member of the Afghani ex-patriot community in the United States, he reflects their conflicted emotions about the home country through Amir, through General Taheri and through Baba.

- Hosseini sets up the various struggles in his book in large-scale epic fashion – there are internal and cultural clashes between the Pashtun and Hazaras juxtaposed to external forces represented by the Russians and the Taliban. But first, Hosseini sets up the small-scale struggles – Amir vs. Hassan; Amir vs. Baba, and so on. By moving between the individual and the national levels, Hosseini highlights the epic nature of the struggle. He wants the reader to understand the thinking behind the activities and then to understand why Afghanistan is not at peace. She cannot be at peace with the world because she has not come to peace with herself.

Relationships   *Brother to Brother; Father and Son; Friends; Afghanis in exile*

- In this country where winning seems to be everything (see Kite, p.57), Hosseini tells us that winning cannot be the end goal. Nothing is simple; everything is complex. For example, winning alone does not bring home the trophy kite; the kite runner must do that. Sacrifice alone won't bring redemption; self-understanding and the courage of conviction must come alongside. Hosseini uses the novel's relationships to reach out to his fellow countrymen, who reside both inside and outside the country, to see whether they can ever be *"good again."* (see Redemption, p.45)

- The relationships of Hassan, Amir, Baba, Rahim Khan and others have been discussed in the characterization section. (p.23-33) We see how each relationship is driven by the character's personality and perspective. A skewed perspective creates a relationship that is not functional. This can be seen most clearly through Amir, whose outlook is completely overshadowed by his unrequited love for his father. This emptiness causes him to both retreat into himself and to lash out at Hassan, again a dual reaction to love.

- The conflicting emotions of love and hate seem to drive all the relationships in the novel. Everyone, including the Afghanis in exile, suffer from these contradictory emotions. Amir never knows whether to be angry at or afraid of Baba, and perhaps Hassan feels the same about Amir. Certainly he has reason to.

> *You can't love a person who lives [in a black and white world] without fearing him too. Maybe even hating him a little.* (p.16)

- The dual elements of love and hate come out of the idea of power. In every instance of power, there are the powerful and the powerless; the executor and the victim. In each of these connections, there is often a sacrificial lamb. (see Lamb, p.61) But, in some cases, the lamb that is being sacrificed has first sacrificed someone else. In this novel, Hosseini shows that sacrifice is the cost of relationship and implies that gaining something means first giving up something else.

    o In this way, the novel underscores the tragedy of human conflict at any and every level of relationship. (see Amir/Hassan p.23) The boys, Hassan and Amir, represent the sibling nature of the Afghan people who should see themselves as brothers instead of fighting.

    o Amir's relationship with Baba is a relationship of power and explores the ways in which one can relate to a person with power. The success of this relationship depends entirely on the perspective of both the powerful and the powerless. Amir is always struggling for the approval that will cement his sense of identity, which Baba feels is his right to give or withhold.

- The irony of this heartbreak becomes clear when later all their roles of power are reversed. (see Irony, p.51) Despite Amir's perception that his father resented him, Baba has really done everything in his power, including leaving Afghanistan, in order to protect and enable Amir's life. Amir understands this on his graduation day from high school. This day belongs to Baba because it justifies for him all of his past struggles. (p.140)

- When Amir looks at Rahim Khan's picture of Hassan and his family, and when he reads Hassan's letter, he sees in Hassan a *"man who thought the world had been good to him."* (p.227) Unlike Amir, Hassan did not seem to reflect on bad memories of the past. He remained deeply respectful and full of love. He has achieved what Amir always sought – dignity and self-confidence. As the novel points out, Hassan has attained what even the Afghanis in exile have not achieved – the peace of a secure identity.

Friendship, Loyalty, Humanity, Compassion

- Assef asks Amir how he can possibly be a friend to Hassan, a Hazara. Amir's own conflicted feelings caused him to almost blurt out, *" he's not my friend! ... [he]'s my servant!"* (p.44) Amir's relationship with Hassan lacks warmth, loyalty, and courage. Their friendship, and to some extent Baba's and Ali's, was indeed more master and servant, although Baba was certainly a more benevolent master.

    Never mind that we spent entire winters flying kites, running kites. Never mind that to me the face of Afghanistan is that of a boy with a thin-boned frame, a shaved head ... perpetually lit by a hairlipped smile. Never mind any of those things because history isn't easy to overcome – Pashtun/Hazara – Sunni/Shi'a. (p.27)

- Friendship requires a loyalty test and the first one comes early in the story. Amir asks Hassan if he would eat dirt as a display of his friendship. (p.57) He asks the question knowing that, although Amir lies to Hassan constantly, Hassan would never lie to him, precisely because he would rather eat dirt than betray Amir. Hassan deflects the test, but they both know that a line has been crossed in their relationship. The second test of loyalty is the pomegranate incident.

Amir pelts Hassan with a blood-red pomegranate and wants Hassan to hit him in return. Instead Hassan smears himself further with the pomegranate's blood, refusing to give Amir the power of the assault, which Amir instigated in an effort to alleviate his guilt. (see Guilt, p.43)

- Their relationship actually ends twice (just like the number of times Afghanistan is wounded in the time frame of this book). After the rape attack, Hassan wants nothing to do with their old activities, nor with Amir. But Hassan's loyalty is so deeply ingrained in him that he eventually returns to rekindle their relationship. But by now, Amir has tasted the fruit of Baba's less-divided attention and resists Hassan by telling him to stop harassing him. Amir's guilt builds and reaches an unbearable point – Hassan must go.

- On page 114, Amir lies once more and sets Hassan up for the theft of his watch. Ali and Hassan leave forever. Baba tries to assert his own loyalty by insisting that Ali and Hassan will remain right there: *"This is his home ... we're his family."* (p.95) But this is Hassan's final sacrifice, *"[he] knew I had betrayed him ..."* (p.111)

- It is Hassan who gives definition and shape to the concept of loyalty. Just before he goes off to retrieve the fallen blue kite, he tells Amir he would do anything for him, *"For you a thousand times over."* (p.71) Amir hears this phrase once more spoken by Farid, his driver in Kabul. Amir passes the test with Farid but is highly aware of the times when he administered the test to Hassan unfairly.

- Amir wins Farid's wary loyalty only after telling him that he has come to seek Sohrab, admitting him to be a blood relative. Farid admires that Amir will find Sohrab and take him out of Afghanistan. Farid's loyalty to Amir is demonstrated by getting them out of Kabul in spite of the danger to himself. He too repeats the oath of loyalty: he would help Amir one thousand times over.

Guilt, Free Will and Determinism

- Throughout the story, Amir is plagued by guilt. He constantly thinks about his actions, is bothered by them, but doesn't seem to know how to resolve the situation until Rahim Khan gives him a way.

- When Hassan returns with the kite, Amir pretends to ask him where he has been. *"Did he know, I knew? And if he knew, then what would I see if I did look in his eyes? Blame? Indignation? Or, God forbid, what I feared most: guileless devotion? That, most of all, I couldn't bear to see."* (p.83) To see a reflection of Hassan's loyalty would simply magnify Amir's guilt.

- As Amir's guilt multiplies, he becomes aware that Rahim Khan also knows the truth.

    > *Little shapes formed behind my eyelids, like hands playing shadows on the wall ... twisted, merged, formed a single image: Hassan's brown corduroy pants discarded on a pile of old bricks in the alley.* (p.89)

- He starts to feel unclean and pierced as though a knife were sticking in his eye, and he realizes that he is cursed. *"I watched Hassan get raped ... I understood the nature of my new curse: I was going to get away with it."* (p.91)

- Amir is just beginning to realize the connection and conflict between his inner desires and his behavior. *"Nothing was free in this world. Maybe Hassan was the price I had to pay, the lamb I had to slay to win Baba. Was it a fair price? ... He was just a Hazara, wasn't he?"* (p.82) He is beginning to understand that to win the prize there will be a cost, many costs and sacrifices. Amir has not only sacrificed Hassan and Ali, but he has sacrificed his own soul. (see Sacrifice, p.61; Redemption, p.45)

- But Amir feels he has no choice. Running throughout the novel is the tension between "free will" and "determinism" (though not necessarily in a religious sense). Hosseini is presenting the concept that there are forces, larger than ourselves, that seem to "cause" us to behave in certain ways, both as individuals and societies.

  > *The curious thing was, I never thought of Hassan and me as friends either ... Because history isn't easy to overcome. Neither is religion. In the end, I was a Pashtun and he was a Hazara, I was Sunni and he was Shi'a, and nothing was ever going to change that. Nothing.* (p.27)

  But in the very next line: *"But we were kids who had learned to crawl together, and no history, ethnicity, society, or religion was going to change that either."*

- Hosseini's position comes down firmly on the side of "free will." He concludes that individuals (and societies) can and should choose to break the tyranny of choices that appear to not be choices, even though he acknowledges the difficulty of acting against those forces. It is the illiterate Hassan who points out the flaw in Amir's first written story:

  > *... if I may ask, why did the man kill his wife? In fact, why did he ever have to feel sad to shed tears? Couldn't he have just smelled an onion?* (p.36)

  He had identified the "Plot Hole," the parts in the script that don't work. This faulty thinking can be found in the "scripts" of both individuals and society, when actions are taken on the false assumption that they are the only and necessary choices. These "scripted" actions can lead to locked and tragic thinking, for example, that there are no reversible solutions for the irreconcilable differences between Sunni and Shi'a Muslims, between the Pashtun and Hazara. Hosseini asks us to speculate that turning the issue around and looking at it from a different perspective might yield different results.

- In an interview with Farhad Azad of afghanmagazine.com, Hosseini says:

    Because these issues of ethnic differences and problems between the different groups continue to hound our society and threaten to undermine our progress toward a better tomorrow, I think – possibly naively – these issues are best dealt with face on. I don't see how we can move forward from our past; how we can overcome our differences, if we refuse to even acknowledge the past and differences.

    The flaw in Amir's thinking is that winning his father's unattainable approval is worth any cost. The real flaw in the general picture is sacrificing the ideal of individual humanity in the mistaken belief that a cost must be paid.

Redemption

- The novel's cry to battle is *"There is a way to be good again."* (p.2) This statement confirms the concept of free will and personal choice as the way to redemption. Amir is plagued with the promise of false redemption, the capture of the kite, the victory of being redeemed in Baba's eyes. What Amir learns much later is that true redemption comes from restoring one's own sense of self-worth and goodness as a human being. Everyone is entitled to be redeemed, even Sanaubar, Hassan's mother.

- Time after time, Amir throws away the chance to set things right. It is the call from the very ill Rahim Khan that offers him a chance to be good again. This is where the story begins. Rahim Khan tells Amir that Hassan laid down his life to protect Amir's property again, one thousand times over. (p.201) Amir imagines Hassan's death, *"his life of unrequited loyalty drifting from him like the wind blown kites he used to chase."* (p.231) Here again is the challenge of Amir's loyalty test. But Amir still does not have the courage and the conscience to take it up. He says no.

- Amir takes his first steps towards redemption only when Rahim Khan tells him that Hassan is his brother. It is this realization of blood and brotherhood that applies to Afghanistan as well.

- Amir is not the only one who needs redemption. Perhaps Rahim Khan, too, suffers from the guilt of actions taken or not taken. He has interfered in Hassan's life, has brought him back to Kabul during troubled times and has put him deliberately in harm's way. He left him vulnerable to certain Taliban assault when he left the small family unprotected in the house.

- Rahim Khan seeks redemption and knows the secret of how to achieve it. He tells Amir that feeling guilt has a good side, because where there is a guilty conscience, there is the possibility of positive action. Bad deeds cannot be undone, but new, good, or better deeds can take their place. The fact that Baba could not acknowledge Hassan as his son led him to build his orphanage so that Afghanistan's other unacknowledged sons could be cared for. Baba forgave himself through this deed. Amir needs to do the same.

- Amir is the only survivor of all the people he was ever close to and loved while he was in Afghanistan. Times have changed and Amir can now acknowledge his socially illegitimate brother. He does so and reaps the benefits. He inherits the wealth, not a monetary wealth, but one that will take a long time to come. This future wealth will come only when Sohrab stops suffering. At the end of the novel, there are glimpses of hope.

So, too, for Afghanistan. The country has not yet been redeemed, but Hosseini is hopeful.

WRITING STYLE AND STRUCTURE

Filmic Quality

Exaggeration and Cliché

Irony

Setting

WRITING STYLE AND STRUCTURE

Filmic Quality

- The novel has the feel of a film. The plot, the characters, the events, and dialogue keep reversing, rewinding as if in a film. The camera pans in to give the reader an initial partial view, then it pulls back to uncover the full view for the greatest impact. We see only bits and parts of Hassan's rape until Amir's final recall on page 89. This style is paralleled in Rahim Khan's visual description of Hassan's murder on page 231, only to be repeated in Amir's dream on page 252.

- Even the climax of the story, the fight between Amir and Assef, is done in the style of a wild-west duel. Assef tells his henchman, *"when it's all done, only one of us will walk out of this room alive ... if it's him, then he's earned his freedom and you let him pass ..."* (p.300) But significantly, it is Sohrab who wins the fight, rightfully avenging his father's death. True to character, Amir is not capable. He is still the boy who needs the help of his "kite runner" to rescue the prize for him. This scene is not within his skill set nor territory. He is much more comfortable with the American half of his life, and here is where the novel takes an optimistic turn. After a severe and lengthy bureaucratic struggle, which Amir finally wins, there is the suggestion that Sohrab will recover and may, in time, be fine.

Exaggeration and Cliché

- At one point in the story, Amir refers to "laaf," the Afghan tendency to exaggeration, which Amir encounters in the flea market when the Afghanis tell their stories, each intended to outdo the other. He refers to it as a national affliction. It is interesting to note that Amir only realizes its nature once he is outside the country looking in. Because of that fact, the reader can feel comfortable that Amir's story is not an exaggeration, and can, therefore, give it the credibility it deserves. By pointing out the presence of exaggeration, Hosseini counters the reader's impatience with the concept.

- Another interesting fact is that Amir focuses on a lecture given by his writing teacher on the necessity and the means by which to avoid clichés (a common literary trap). Amir argues that clichés are a necessary and positive tool for writers because clichés represent common truths that also comfort readers, especially when they are in unfamiliar territory. Hosseini's novel is riddled with clichés, always a risky thing for a brave author to do. But Hosseini points out that there is a greater danger of applying stereotypical misconceptions even to this storytelling experience, and as he does so, he reassures the readers that what they are reading is not unusual or foreign. The reader can bring to the novel his/her own personal and similar human experiences and emotions.

- Pathetic fallacy is a literary technique which juxtaposes the outer physical world with the inner psychological one, usually involving the weather. In the hands of an inexperienced writer, pathetic fallacy can be a cliché. It rains the summer that Ali and Hassan leave, matching the tears that Ali and Baba shed for the end of their lives as they know it. (p.114) There are many other instances of compassionate weather descriptions in the story.

Irony

- Along with the idea of exaggeration and cliché, Hosseini points out the role of irony in telling an important story. Writers use irony to highlight and emphasize the difference between the reader's perception and the author's intention of an event or statement or character. This can be seen in the book's opening sentence: *"I became what I am today at the age of twelve, on a frigid overcast day in the winter of 1975."* (p.1)

- While it is true that this day was a hugely significant turning point in Amir's life, it is equally not true. He becomes what he is today at many other times in the novel, because of the influence of his relationship with a very demanding yet distant father, as well as through the times that he acted in a cowardly way towards Hassan. He did not protect Hassan adequately and he lied about him several times to protect himself. *"But he never told on me. Never told that the mirror, like shooting walnuts at the neighbor's dog, was always my idea."* (p.4) Sometimes the lies were of omission, rather than actual verbal lies.

- Ironically, Amir uses irony in his own story. (p.33) In his story, the protagonist gains riches at the expense of his wife's life, so he is unable to enjoy his wealth. The double irony is that the man was happiest when he was poor. There had not been a need for the pearls in the first place. This fits with another well-known cliché – you don't know what you have until it's gone. This irony seems to point to a parallel in Amir's own life. His triumphant win of the kite tournament, added to by the capture of the blue kite, was a pyrrhic one, a victory that is defined in the dictionary as *"won at too great a cost to be of use to the victor."*

- Amir learns nothing from his own story. He so desperately wants his father's love that he sacrifices Hassan to get it.

Setting

- The novel takes Afghanistan through three stages in its recent history as experienced by Amir: the transition of revolution, Soviet occupation, and the Taliban takeover. Amir tells us that the Afghanistan he knew came to an official end, first in April of 1978, and then again when the Russian tanks entered in December of 1979. The sounds of invasion were *"foreign sounds to us then. The generation of Afghan children whose ears would know nothing but the sounds of bombs and gunfire was not yet born."* (p.39)

- Like many fellow Afghanis, Amir and Baba escape in 1981. The description of the fuel truck and the near-rape incident of a fellow traveler may be a pale comparison to what many refugees experience in their own personal and similar situations. (p.129) The year 1989, when the Taliban first came to power after the expulsion of the Russians, *"... should have been a glory time for Afghans, ... instead they faced civil war, Afghans and Mujahedin."* (p.193, 194) It was also coincidentally the same year as the fall of the Berlin wall and the riot in Tiananmen square.

- Hosseini's descriptions of Afghanistan and America are vividly described by Amir. The contrast is strong and effective. Afghanistan is a place where *"mines were planted like seeds of death and children buried in rock-piled graves, Kabul had become a city of ghosts for me."* On the other hand, *"America was different. America was a river, roaring along, unmindful of the past. I could wade into this river, let my sins drown to the bottom, let the waters carry me someplace far. Someplace with no ghosts, no memories, and no sins."* (p.144)

- Hosseini takes us to the setting of the flea market, a metaphorical place where the old and new mingle, where one person's memories become the next person's trophies. A place where the displaced items of one's life can be looked at again with new perspective. At the flea market we meet displaced people like General Taheri, who waits to be rediscovered.

- The settings of the novel as a whole bring back memories and discuss the wish for memories to be obliterated or modified. This is important and ironic, because in the end, memories are the only possible foundation for change through insight. If it were not for the memories that Amir carries with him (the good ones and the bad), he would not have been convinced to go back to Kabul to rescue Sohrab. Here again is a place which marks the person Amir is to become.

- In America, Amir finishes and publishes his first novel about a father/son relationship. *"... there was so much goodness in my life. So much happiness. I wondered whether I deserved any of it."* (p.192)

SYMBOLS

Kite

Cleft

Dreams

Lamb, Sacrifice

Blood

SYMBOLS

There are many symbols in the novel, which reflect Amir's use of cliché, but the novel would not be the same without them.

Kite

> *Every winter, districts in Kabul held a kite-fighting tournament. If you were a boy living in Kabul, the day of the tournament was undeniably the highlight of the cold season ... In Kabul, fighting kites was a little like going to war.* (p.52)

- For Amir, this war takes many forms – the tension of the battle for the actual kite, the sadness of his inner battle over not protecting Hassan, the battle for Baba's attention and praise, and the battle over whether to get involved in the rescue of Sohrab.

- The book opens with the first lovely image of a *"pair of kites ...soaring in the sky ... [dancing] high above the trees ... floating side by side."* (p.1) This is the relationship between Hassan and Amir, a relationship that is never properly grounded. They float next to each other, bumping up against each other accidentally or manipulated purposely. They are a perfect team, the kite-fighter and the kite runner, each a champion in his own field. But the team is doomed to failure because Amir refuses to acknowledge Hassan's talent, and because of Hassan's subordinate role in Amir's life. The kite is the key to Baba's heart and Hassan is holding it when he is cornered by Assef. (p.75) Amir sacrifices Hassan's heart for Baba's.

- Kites are the only thing that Amir and Baba have in common. Their personalities, hopes, dreams and wishes are so different, that *"[kites are] the one paper-thin slice of intersection between spheres of their existence."* (p.52) Amir and Baba finally come to a less-than-perfect, but mutual understanding, but the struggle is long and hard.

- Kite-fighting has a political parallel. The crossing of kite lines metaphorically represents the crossing of political and non-political lines, with few guidelines. In Amir's neighborhood, *"the Hindi kid would soon learn what the British learned earlier in the century, and what the Russians would eventually learn by the late 1980's: that the Afghans are an independent people. Afghans cherish custom but abhor rules."* (p.55) Kite-flying and fighting have only one rule – winning. This makes the last fight scene between Assef and Amir closer to being believable.

- To bring home the last fallen kite is to bring home the trophy of honor. It is the reason Amir is so desperate to win, and will go to any lengths, even evil ones, to do so. Amir once betrayed Hassan to get and keep this trophy, although the aftermath of the win was very difficult. Now Sohrab is the fallen kite and winning the fight with Assef will still not be enough. It is equally challenging for Amir to bring Sohrab home to the U.S. Both Sohrab and Hassan bleed in the process.

Cleft

- Hassan was a beautiful boy with a *"face like a Chinese doll chiseled from hardwood,"* but with a *"... cleft lip, just left of midline, where the Chinese doll maker's instrument may have slipped, or perhaps he had simply grown tired and careless."* (p.3) When Baba gives Hassan the gift of healing, surgery to fix his cleft lip, Amir is jealous. *"I wished I too had some kind of scar that would beget Baba's sympathy. It wasn't fair."* (p.50) Amir does have a scar, only his is on his heart, invisible even to himself.

- During Amir's fight with Assef, he is hit in the mouth. The impact cuts his upper lip, *"clean down the middle ... like a harelip."* (p.312) Now his scar is visible and can begin to be healed.

- Hassan's cleft lip is a symbol for the genetic split in Afghan society – the two faces of Afghanistan. Although there are other demographic divisions, for the sake of this novel Hosseini is interested only in the differences between the Pashtun and the Hazara.

- Another example of cleft is the split in Afghan history, which occurred when Amir was a boy. It is the time of the Russian occupation, which split life between the glory years of Amir's boyhood and the Taliban takeover. (p.39)

Dreams

- The morning of the kite tournament, Hassan has a dream about a lake and a monster. Amir is mean to him about the dream. But perhaps Hassan knew that Amir was nervous about the day's event and invented the story of the dream. *"Hassan understood I was just nervous. Hassan always understood about me."* (p.64)

- Hassan is often insightful and sensitive; in fact, he is everything Amir would like to be but isn't. *"How could I be such an open book to him when half the time, I had no idea what was mulling around in his head? I was the one who went to school ... read, write ... I was the smart one."* (p.65, 66)

- Dreams have a tendency to drift into nightmares just as a kite drifts from being the highest and then falls – Amir returning to Afghanistan is like a *"man who awakens in his own house and finds the furniture rearranged."* (p.236)

- During the attack on Hassan, Amir is lost in a memory/dream/nightmare. *"A hand reaches out for me. I see deep, parallel gashes across the palm, blood dripping, staining the snow. I take the hand and suddenly the snow is gone ... I look up and see the clear sky is filled with kites ..."* (p.79) After Hassan's rape, Amir recalls Hassan's water dream and realizes that he is the monster grabbing Hassan by the ankles. (p.91)

- Amir becomes an insomniac after the attack and begins having continuous and intense bad dreams. As a result of this psychological pressure, and in an effort to stop the dreams, Amir sets up the scheme which implicates Hassan.

- Upon finding out about Hassan's death, Amir resumes his nightmares in which he sees the killing over and over. This is his guilt, his limbo. *"Somewhere over there, the blindfolded man from my dream had died a needless death. Once, over those mountains, I had made a choice."* The choice, of course, was the sacrifice of Hassan. (p.253)

Lamb and Sacrifice

- When Assef rapes Hassan, Amir catches *"a glimpse of [Hassan's] face. Saw the resignation in it ... It was the look of the lamb."* (p.81)

- Amir is a coward who willingly sacrifices Hassan for his selfish goals. *"Maybe Hassan was the price I had to pay, the lamb I had to slay to win Baba."* (p.82) But Hassan makes the final sacrifice. Hassan defends Amir, all the while knowing that Amir has betrayed him. This betrayal pushes Hassan and his father out of Baba's house. (p.111)

- Strangely, it is Amir who feels that he has always sacrificed himself for Baba's attentions. He feels he has denied himself his deepest wishes, for example, to freely pursue his love for English and writing. As he goes off to university to study English, he convinces himself that he *"[doesn't] want to sacrifice for Baba anymore. The last time I had done that, I had damned myself."* (p.142) Amir deludes himself into thinking and feeling that he is the one who sacrifices himself for Baba by trying to become the son he thinks Baba wants. What he doesn't know is that Baba wants two sons, not one or the other. Is it Baba he blames or himself?

- Amir cannot deal with the aftermath of the rape and with his own reactions. He comes to the irrational conclusion that if he can sacrifice Hassan and send him away, he would rid himself of all his problems. This is a common response of all bullies, but the real issue is that he knows that Hassan knows that Amir has betrayed him. Hassan's final act of loyalty and friendship is to admit to the theft of Amir's new watch and to leave.

- Nothing can compare to the living nightmare in which Amir finds himself on his return to Afghanistan. At the Ghazi stadium soccer game, he watches the half-time show. It is the application of the Taliban's version of Shari'a justice – *"every sinner must be punished in a manner befitting his sin. ... These are believed to be the words of God."* (p.283) A couple is charged with adultery and stoned to death. They have been sacrificed for the "good" of the country.

Blood

- The image of blood represents a number of things, specifically Hassan's rape. More generally, the blood spilled in the name of Afghanistan represents the notion of sacrifice. Hassan's execution can be traced back to the pomegranate incident.

    What would you do if I hit you with this?" I said, tossing the fruit up and down ...

    The color fell from his face ... I hurled the pomegranate at him. It struck him in the chest, exploded in a spray of red pulp ...

    ... when I finally stopped, exhausted and panting, Hassan was smeared in red like he'd been shot by a firing squad. I fell to my knees, tired, spent, frustrated. (p.97)

    Hassan is Amir's sacrifice on the altar of Baba and Afghanistan.

- The image extends to Amir's many birthday gifts following his kite tournament triumph. *"I didn't want any of it – it was all blood money. Baba would have never thrown me a party like this if I hadn't won the tournament."* (p.107) Amir sees everything in these terms. Even his red new bicycle reminds him of blood – the blood he saw on the ground after Hassan's attack.

- Blood as a death image is repeated in Baba's bloodstained phlegm. He was ill with cancer and dying. In a way, it is Baba's passing that releases Amir only slightly from his lifelong struggle for redemption.

Baba's death allows Amir to finally concentrate on his real abilities, not the ones he imagines he must have for Baba's sake.

- Blood, however, is not only a death image; it also represents the stuff of life. Amir and Soraya try unsuccessfully to have a child. When they think about adopting, the idea of continuing a bloodline gets in the way. As the General tells them, *"[blood] is a powerful thing ... and when you adopt, you don't know whose blood you're bringing into your house."* (p.198) There is both truth and reprehension in this statement. On one hand, this philosophy justifies the categorization of people in terms of their bloodlines; on the other hand, adopting a child is a serious undertaking and genetics does play a major role in family connections. For Amir, remaining childless feels like his ultimate punishment.

- Blood is what prevents Baba from affirming Hassan as his son, due to the social environment of the time. He simply cannot claim an illegitimate child, let alone an illegitimate Hazara one. But in Amir's dream about Assef, Amir begins to conceptualize that regardless of individual personality, culture or conflict, and as distasteful as it might seem to be, all Afghanis must begin to consider themselves as one. *"We're the same, you and I, [Assef] was saying. "You nursed with him, but you're my twin."* (p.322)

- The final blood image is enmeshed in Sohrab's attempted suicide. Amir's final steps toward redemption come at this moment. *"My hands are stained with Hassan's blood; I pray God doesn't let them get stained with the blood of his boy too."* (p.364)

LAST THOUGHTS

LAST THOUGHTS

- It would seem that the direct causes of Amir's weakness of character come out of Baba's pride, his lack of honesty and his forcefulness. This bear of a man causes havoc not only in Amir's life, but in the lives of all the characters, in one way or another. If Baba had more of his own definition of moral courage, his openness would strengthen Amir and enable him to behave very differently. Perhaps the outcome then, for Hassan, would be different. But it is not for the reader to judge, because Hosseini makes clear that Baba is the person he is because of how the social structure and political climate of the country created him. Hosseini's conclusion is for Amir and the country not to dwell so much on the past, but to look to the future and simply carry on from there.

- There seems to be the suggestion that pride is both empowering and destructive. Baba's arrogance takes away Amir's ability to develop a sense of self-pride. If the reader continues with this metaphor, Hosseini points out that pride in one's country is a motivating factor, while arrogance which leads to cultural superiority can destroy the fabric of one's environment.

- It must be mentioned that Hosseini is also concerned with the difference in cultural perceptions. Westerners may not accept or understand his Afghani perspective, so he attempts to explain it in terms of a very American phenomenon – the movie. He talks about Americans not liking to be told the end of a film – they want to discover it on their own. He counters this with the Afghani perspective.

> *In Afghanistan, the ending was all that mattered. When Hassan and I came home after watching a Hindi film ... what [everyone] wanted to know was this: Did the Girl in the film find happiness? Did the Guy ... fulfill his dreams, or was he ... doomed to wallow in failure?* (p.376)

Here Amir reflects on the end of his own story. From one point of view, his story's ending is not a happy one – his close friends and family are dead, he is childless. From another standpoint, he has successfully brought Sohrab to America, making the best of a bad situation. Perhaps a happy ending, as is present in fictional stories, is elusive in real life. A happy ending is usually an ambiguous affair, but the goal is to keep trying. The novel's final scene is the reverse of Amir and Hassan's kite running days. Amir is kite runner to Sohrab. This is his final redeeming act, his way to find goodness and redemption.

FROM THE NOVEL

Quotes

FROM THE NOVEL...

Memorable Quotes from the Text of The Kite Runner

PAGE 1. ... I went for a walk along Spreckels Lake on the northern edge of Golden Gate Park. The early-afternoon sun sparkled on the water where dozens of miniature boats sailed, propelled by a crisp breeze. Then I glanced up and saw a pair of kites, red with long blue tails, soaring in the sky. They danced high above the trees ... over the windmills, gloating side by side like a pair of eyes looking down on San Francisco, the city I now call home. And suddenly Hassan's voice whispered in my head: For you, a thousand times over. Hassan the harelipped kite runner.

PAGE 13. Lore has it my father once wrestled a black bear in Baluchistan with his bare hands. If the story had been about anyone else, it would have been dismissed as *laaf*, that Afghan tendency to exaggerate ... But no one ever doubted the veracity of any story about Baba. And if they did, well, Baba did have those three parallel scars coursing a jagged path down his back ... in [my] dreams, I can never tell Baba from the bear.

PAGE 19. "... no matter what the mullah teaches, there is only one sin, only one. And that is theft. Every other sin is a variation of theft." ... Baba heaved a sigh of impatience. That stung too, because he was not an impatient man. I remembered all the times he didn't come home until after dark ... though I knew full well he was at the construction site, overlooking this, supervising that. Didn't that take patience? I already hated all the kids he was building the orphanage for; sometimes I wished they'd all died along with their parents.

PAGE 30. Sitting cross-legged, sunlight and shadows of pomegranate leaves dancing on his face, Hassan absently plucked blades of grass from the ground as I read him stories he couldn't read for himself. That Hassan would grow up illiterate like Ali and most Hazaras had been decided the minute he had been born ... after all, what use did a servant have for the written word?

PAGE 41. If you were a kid living in the Wazir Akbar Khan section of Kabul, you knew about Assef and his famous stainless-steel brass knuckles, hopefully not through personal experience ... His well-earned reputation for savagery preceded him on the streets ... Years later, I learned an English word for the creature that Assef was, a word for which a good Farsi equivalent does not exist: "sociopath."

PAGE 46. For the next couple of years, the words *economic development* and *reform* danced on a lot of lips in Kabul. The constitutional monarchy had been abolished, replaced by a republic, led by a president of the republic ... And for the most part ... life went on as before.

PAGE 54, 55. The kite-fighting tournament was an old winter tradition in Afghanistan. It started early in the morning on the day of the contest and didn't end until only the winning kite flew in the sky ... Every kite-fighter had an assistant – in my case, Hassan – who held the spool and fed the line ... The real fun began when a kite was cut. That was where the kite runners came in, those kids who chased the windblown kite drifting through the neighborhoods until it came spiralling down ... when a kite runner had his hands on a kite, no one could take if from him. That wasn't a rule. That was custom.

PAGE 82. I stopped watching, turned away from the alley. Something warm was running down my wrist. I blinked, saw I was still biting down on my fist, hard enough to draw blood from the knuckles. I realized something else. I was weeping ...

I had one last chance to make a decision. One final opportunity to decide who I was going to be. I could step into that alley, stand up for Hassan – the way he'd stood up for me all those times in the past – and accept whatever would happen to me. Or I could run.

In the end, I ran.

PAGE 111. Baba came right out and asked. "Did you steal that money? Did you steal Amir's watch, Hassan?"

Hassan's reply was a single word ... "Yes."

I flinched, like I'd been slapped ... [I had] another understanding: Hassan knew. He knew I'd seen everything in that alley, that I'd stood there and done nothing. He knew I had betrayed him and yet he was rescuing me once again, maybe for the last time. I loved him in that moment, loved him more than I'd ever loved anyone, and I wanted to tell them all that I was the snake in the grass, the monster in the lake ... And I would have told, except that a part of me was glad.

PAGE 119. What was I doing on this road in the middle of the night? I should have been in bed, under my blanket, a book with dog-eared pages at my side. This had to be a dream. Tomorrow morning, I'd wake up, peek out the window: No grim-faced Russian soldiers patrolling the sidewalks, no tanks rolling up and down the streets of my city ... no rubble, no curfews, no Russian Army Personnel Carriers weaving through the bazaars ... This was no dream. As if on cue, a MiG suddenly screamed past overhead.

PAGE 132. Baba loved the idea of America ... It was living in America that gave him an ulcer.

PAGE 135, 136. "My father is still adjusting to life in America," I said ... I wanted to tell them that, in Kabul, we snapped a tree branch and used it as a credit card. Hassan and I would take the wooden stick to the bread maker. He'd carve notches on our stick with his knife ... At the end of the month, my father paid him for the number of notches on the stick. That was it. No questions. No ID.

PAGE 165. "I wish you'd give the chemo a chance, Baba." ... A look of disgust swept across his rain-soaked face ... "You're twenty-two years old, Amir! A grown man! .... What's going to happen to you, you say? All those years, that's what I was trying to teach you, how to never have to ask that question."

PAGE 171. Baba wet his hair and combed it back. I helped him into a clean white shirt and knotted his tie for him, noting the two inches of empty space between the collar button and Baba's neck. I thought of all the empty spaces Baba would leave behind when he was gone, and I made myself think of something else.

PAGE 178. Baba spent $35,000, nearly the balance of his life savings, on the *awroussi*, the wedding ceremony.

PAGE 180. I remember sitting on the sofa, set on the stage like a throne, Soraya's hand in mine, as three hundred or so faces looked on ... I remember wishing Rahim Khan were there ... And I remember wondering if Hassan too had married. And if so, whose face he had seen in the mirror under the veil? Whose henna-painted hands had he held?

PAGE 183, 184. As words from the Koran reverberated through the room, I thought of the old story of Baba wrestling a black bear in Baluchistan. Baba had wrestled bears his whole life. Losing his young wife. Raising a son by himself. Leaving his beloved homeland ... Poverty. Indignity. In the end, a bear had come that he couldn't best. But even then, he had lost on his own terms ... I realized how much of who I was, what I was, had been defined by Baba and the marks he had left on people's lives. My whole life, I had been "Baba's son." Now he ... couldn't show me the way anymore; I'd have to find it on my own ... The thought terrified me.

PAGE 224, 225 I told you how we all celebrated in 1996 when the Taliban rolled in and put an end to the daily fighting ... A few weeks later, the Taliban banned kite fighting. And two years later, in 1998, they massacred the Hazaras in Mazar-i-Sharif.

PAGE 226. It hit me again, the enormity of what I had done that winter and that following summer. The names rang in my head: Hassan, Sohrab, Ali, Farzana, and Sanaubar.

PAGE 238. Rahim Khan said I'd always been too hard on myself ... But I had driven Hassan and Ali out of the house. Was it too farfetched to imagine that things might have turned out differently if I hadn't? Maybe Baba would have brought them along to America. Maybe Hassan would have had a home of his own now, a job, a family, a life in a country where no one cared that he was a Hazara ... I can't go to Kabul, I had said to Rahim Khan. I have a wife in America, a home, a career, and a family. But how could I pack up and go back home when my actions may have cost Hassan a chance at those very same things?

PAGE 254. ... I thanked Wahid for his hospitality ... His three sons were standing in the doorway watching us. The little one was wearing the watch - it dangled around his twiggy wrist ... Earlier that morning, when I was certain no one was looking, I did something I had done twenty-six years earlier: I planted a fistful of crumpled money under a mattress.

PAGE 259, 260. The red Toyota pickup truck idled past us. A handful of stern-faced young men sat on their haunches in the cab, Kalashnikovs slung on their shoulders. They all wore beards and black turbans. One of them, a dark-skinned man in his early twenties with thick, knitted eyebrows twirled a whip in his hand and rhythmically swatted the side of the truck with it. His roaming eyes fell on me. Held my gaze. I'd never felt so naked in my entire life.

PAGE 281. I remembered how green the playing field grass had been in the '70s when Baba used to bring me to soccer games here. Now the pitch was a mess. There were holes and craters everywhere, most notable a pair of deep holes in the ground behind the south-end goalposts. And there was no grass at all, just dirt. When the two teams finally took the field ... and play began, it became difficult to follow the ball in the clouds of dust kicked up by the players. Young, whip-toting Talibs roamed the aisles, striking anyone who cheered too loudly.

PAGE 316. Amir jan, I know how hard your father was on you when you were growing up. I saw how you suffered and yearned for his affections, and my heart bled for you. But your father was a man torn between two halves, Amir jan: you and Hassan. He loved you both, but he could not love Hassan the way he longed to, openly, and as a father. So he took it out on you instead – Amir, the socially legitimate half, the half that represented the riches he had inherited ... When he saw you, he saw himself. And his guilt ... Your father, like you, was a tortured soul, Amir jan ...

... I know that in the end, God will forgive. He will forgive your father, me, and you too. I hope you can do the same. Forgive your father if you can. Forgive me if you wish. But, most important, forgive yourself.

PAGE 390, 391. The green kite hesitated. Held position. Then shot down.

... "Do you want me to run that kite for you?"

His Adam's apple rose and fell as he swallowed. The wind lifted his hair. I thought I saw him nod. "For you, a thousand times over," I heard myself say.

Then I turned and ran.

ACKNOWLEDGEMENTS

ACKNOWLEDGEMENTS

"Afghanistan" The New Encyclopedia Brittanica, Vol. 13. Chicago: Encyclopedia Britannica Inc., 2002.

Azad, Farhad. "Dialogue with Khaled Hosseini". afghanmagazine.com June, 2004.

Ellis, Deborah. "Afghanistan: dream and nightmare". *Globe and Mail*, April 16, 2005.

Marchand, Philip. "A Childhood in Afghanistan". *Toronto Star*, August 5, 2003.

Otfinoski, Steven. "Afghanistan: Nations in Transition". New York: Facts on File, Inc., 2005.

Sadat, Mir Hekmatullah. "Afghan History: kite flying, kite running and kite banning". afghanmagazine.com June, 2004.

Salahuddin, Sayed. (Kabul). "Afghanistan's election results finally released". The *Globe and Mail*, November 14, 2005.